For my son John · RT
For Tom Stoffer · KP

Oxford University Press, Walton Street, Oxford OX2 6DP

Oxford New York Toronto
Delhi Bombay Calcutta Madras Karachi
Kuala Lumpur Singapore Hong Kong Tokyo
Nairobi Dar es Salaam Cape Town
Melbourne Auckland Madrid

and associated companies in
Berlin Ibadan

Oxford is a trade mark of Oxford University Press

Text © Robin Tzannes 1994
Illustrations © Korky Paul 1994

First published 1994
First published paperback 1995

ISBN 0 19 279978 9 (hardback)
ISBN 0 19 272290 5 (paperback)

A CIP catalogue record for this book is available from the
British Library

Printed in Hong Kong

MOOKIE GOES FISHING

Written by Robin Tzannes
Illustrated by Korky Paul

OXFORD UNIVERSITY PRESS
Oxford Toronto Melbourne

One day Mookie's father was getting ready to go fishing.

'Oh, Daddy, may I come too?' asked Mookie. 'Please, Daddy, may I? Please?'

His father smiled but shook his head.

'No, son,' he replied. 'I'm afraid you're too young. You'll talk too much and scare away the fish. You'll fidget and fuss and get in my way.'

Then, seeing the tears in Mookie's eyes, he patted his head kindly and added, 'Maybe when you're older...'

Then he picked up his fishing tackle and set off.

Mookie went for a walk, feeling sad.

'I wish I were big enough to go fishing,' he said to himself.

As he walked, he began to feel angry.

'I'm *not* too young! I could sit still! I wouldn't scare the fish away!'

He kept on walking, and soon he reached the river.

That gave Mookie an idea.

'I *will* go fishing!' he said. 'Then they'll see!'

Mookie climbed up on to a big rock and looked down into the water.

He could see little fish swimming around among the weeds.

How could he catch one?

'First I'll need a fishing rod,' he decided.

So he went into the woods and searched among the fallen branches for a stick that looked just right.

Soon he found one and brought it back to his big rock.

Mookie sat down, the way he'd seen his father sitting, and held the stick out over the water.

He waited. And waited.

Nothing happened.

At last he remembered something.

'Line!' shouted Mookie. 'Of course, I need a line.'

Now, Mookie was the kind of boy who always had pockets full of treasure.

He emptied them out on to the big rock.

There were two plastic buttons, a bit of blue crayon, some pieces of broken alarm clock, a clam shell, a wad of tin foil, three marbles, a mess of orange peel, a rusted toy car, a square of very stale peanut butter sandwich, a smooth grey stone... and a tangle of string.

This he untangled, and tied on to his stick, letting the end dangle into the water.

Mookie waited patiently.

Sometimes a little fish would swim up to the string, sniff at it, and swim away.

How were they ever to get *caught*?

Mookie thought and thought, until he had the answer.

'Hook!' he cried. 'I need a hook on the end of the string!'

Now, Mookie was the kind of boy who was always tearing his clothes. And most of the time, there were safety pins to hold things together.

He hurriedly checked his shirt, and then his shorts.

Sure enough, in the hem of his left leg was a safety pin.

Mookie bent it into the shape of a hook. Then he tied it on to his string, and let it drop into the water.

Mookie lay down quietly and waited.

The little fish darted in and out among the river grass, but hardly seemed to notice his hook.

While Mookie watched them he began to wonder: how could he make the fish bite the hook?

And then he remembered.

'Worms! Fish *love* worms!'

Now, Mookie was the kind of boy who was especially good at finding worms.

He ran up the river bank and turned over a few of the right kind of rocks.

Soon he had a fistful of pink and juicy worms.

He chose the biggest, most delicious-looking one, and very carefully put it on to his hook.

Then he lowered it gently into the water, picked up his rod, and peered into the river.

All the small fish had gathered around the wriggling worm, sniffing it excitedly.

One brave little fish opened his mouth to take a bite . . . but just at that moment a long, dark shadow came rippling over the weeds.

All the little fish darted away in fright.

Out from a dark cave deep in the river came a big, fat, green-spotted fish. He swam slowly, slowly up to the worm, sniffed it once, then sniffed it again.

Then he opened his enormous mouth . . .

. . . and suddenly chomped down on the worm — hook, line, and all!

The fish was heavy, but Mookie held on to the rod and pulled with all his might.

At last the big green-spotted fish flopped up on to the rock.

'I *knew* I could catch a fish!' cried Mookie.

Then he set off for home, feeling very happy.

Mookie ran up to the house, shouting, 'Mummy, Mummy, come look at this fish!'

'My, what a size!' said his mother. 'Did Daddy catch it?'

'No, he didn't,' smiled Mookie.

'Well, who gave it to you then?' she asked.

'Nobody gave it to me!' replied Mookie.

'You couldn't have bought it…'

'Nope.'

'Mookie,' said his mother quietly, 'I *know* you didn't steal this fish…'

'Of course I didn't steal it!' cried Mookie. 'I caught it! All by myself! And oh, Mummy! Isn't he beautiful? And isn't he *HUGE*???'

Just then Mookie's father arrived, muttering to himself.

'Didn't catch a thing! The fish just weren't biting! *No one* could have caught *anything* today!'

Then he saw Mookie's giant fish. 'Where in the world did you get that?'

Mookie told him the whole story. When he was done, his father beamed with pride.

'Mookie,' he said, 'you are a natural-born fisherman! I'd love to see how you do it. How about taking me with you, next time you go fishing?'

'I don't know,' said Mookie. 'You might talk and scare away the fish.'

'No,' said his father, 'I won't talk.'

'And you won't fidget and fuss?' asked Mookie. 'And get in my way?'

'No,' said his father, 'I won't fidget and fuss.'

'Well,' said Mookie, 'I guess you're *old* enough . . .'

Then he started to giggle, and his father did too.

'Yes, Daddy!' laughed Mookie. 'I'll be *happy* to take you with me, next time I go fishing!'

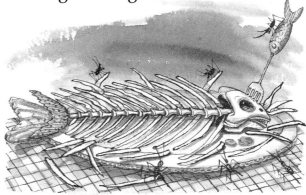